Yackety Zac

by Chris Gurney *illustrated by* Ross Kinnaird

OneTree HOUSE

For Olivia and Noah, who can tell everyone this story is about their Dad — CG

To Hannah. Please don't stop yacking — RK

First published in 2018 by **OneTree House**
PO Box 11745, Ellerslie, Auckland 1542, New Zealand

Text © Chris Gurney, 2018
Illustration © Ross Kinnaird, 2018

ISBN: 978-0-9951064-5-1

All rights reserved. No part of this publication may be reproduced or transmitted in any form or by any means, electronic, mechanical or digital, including photocopying, recording, storage in any information retrieval system, or otherwise, without prior written permission of the publisher.

A catalogue record for this book is available from the National Library of New Zealand

6 5 4 3 2 1   8 9/1   0 1 2 /2

Zachary Black went **yackety-yak**

as he entered the world like a shot.

"Greetings!" he called.

"Nice meeting you all... need a bath and a feed on the spot!"

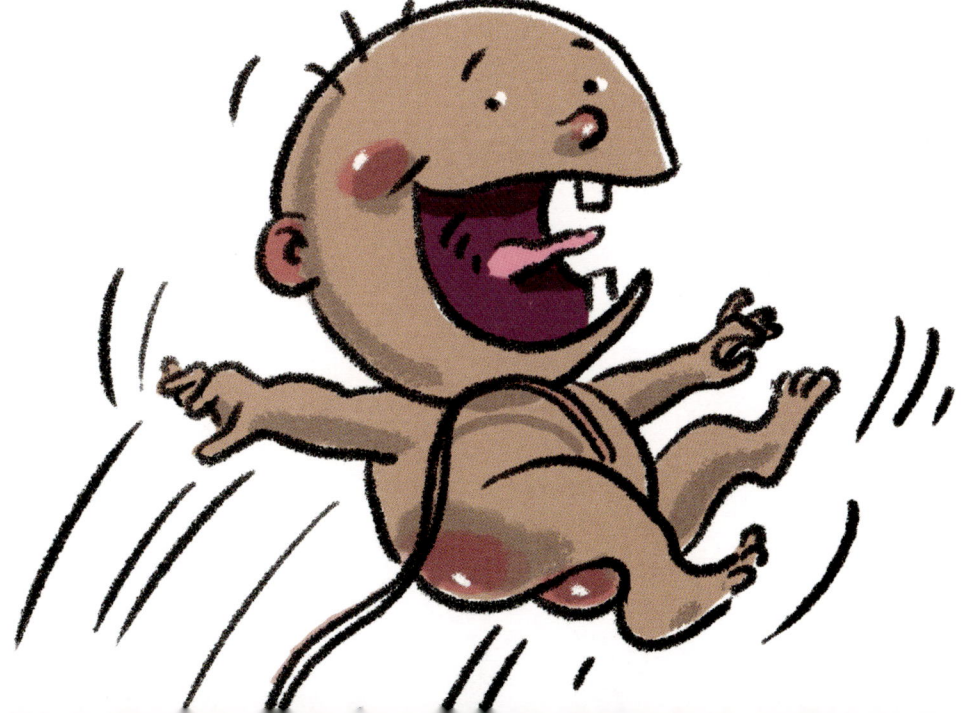

Yackety Yak Yak Yackety

The doctor gasped
and swallowed his mask.
The midwife
quite forgot her task.
Dad took a gulp
from his coffee flask,
while Mum tied her sheet in a knot.

Yak
Yak

Later

Out in his pram
with his doting Gran,
Zachary **yackety-yakked.**

"Faster please, kick up those knees, we need to get home for my snack!"

"Watch out Mrs Bly!"

he called, whizzing by.
Her mouth dropped open
and in buzzed a fly.

Down by the swings
and the slip-slidey things,
the mothers would meet
with their brood.

Yackety-yak

went the mothers and Zac,
while all of the babies just cooed.

"I've learned to crawl, and can catch a ball! I drew with crayon on the wall!"

"I'm pretty smart though I'm only small!"

Yacked Zac, in a braggarty mood.

Then later

Proud Mrs Black,
and her husband Jack,
were pleased
with their son's clever chatter.
But as time went by,
you would hear them both sigh,
for all day and all night
Zac would natter.

Yackety Yak Yak Yackety Yak

Zac started school
and found it most cruel
that kids don't talk
where the teachers rule.
"To blabberty blab in class
is not cool."

"Oh Dear!"
moaned his mum,
"What's the matter?"

Mum took young Zac
to see Doctor Mac . . .

Yak

Yackety

Yak

who peered down his throat
with a light.

Yackety Yak

Yackety

He looked up his nose
and under his toes.

Then measured his weight
and his height.

Yackety Yak Yackety Yak Yak

"My dear Mrs Black,"
began Doctor Mac,
"I know what is wrong
with your small son Zac.
He's got an attack
of tongue **Clicky-Clack**,
which is terribly hard to put right!
To be a success,
Zac must learn to talk less
and **LISTEN** to what others say.
Or his ears may come loose,
if they're not put to use,
and blow off on the next windy day!"

Out of his bag,
Doctor Mac pulled a flag,
a new roll of bandage,
a car racing mag,
a packet of sandwiches starting to sag,
and a sack that was tatty and grey.

The Doc, looking stern,
said with concern,
"Both of you have to agree,
if we're to be sure of achieving a cure,
you'll follow the rules set by me.

Each time young Zac goes **yackety-yak**
as the words tumble out
he must fetch them all back
and drop them into
this Clackety Sack . . .

then gobble them all up for tea."

Zachary Black went yackety-yak

for it seemed that he just couldn't stop.

Then he stowed all his words

in the Clackety Sack and gave it a twist at the top.

For dinner he knew there was no meaty stew.
He counted the words as he started to chew.
There were thirty thousand, nine hundred and two!
Zachary thought he would pop!

Zachary Black went blabberty-blab,
and he felt kind of sick in his tum.
'The words made him gag, rolling flibberty flab,
like stones in a rackety drum.

Next night in his dish, instead of fried fish,
were umpteen words that were far from delish.
His stomach churned in a sickening swish...

"NO MORE YACKETY!"

Zac yelled to his mum.

And so...

Zac learned to choose
the right words to use
and to listen to what others say.
At last there was peace,
the yackety ceased.
(Plus his ears never did blow away!)

For tea, Zac was pleased
to see meatballs and cheese,
fluffy white mash,
and a small side of peas,
with nothing that looked like those old **ABC**'s.

Yackety yak don't come back!